Life is nothing without trust, love, and respect, so respect each and every person in your life.

"Life of Nidhi"

Colorful and Meaningful life…

"Life is like a balloon; we don't know when it will blast away, so until it has air inside it, be yourself, enjoy yourself, spread happiness, and kush raho."

Roles:

Nidhi:

Beautiful, kindhearted, innocent, and talented, she is a talented girl whose mind is full of dreams, good thoughts, and positivity—Nidhi (BBA).

She has a small and cute family, which includes her father, mother, and her granny. Her father is a CEO of a big company (businessman).

But she has a big friend group.

Childhood friends:

- Anjali (BBA).

- Arjun (engineer)

- Anusha (Doctor)

- Ankit (BBA)

- Arpita (Engineer).

- Ajay (Engineer)

PU friends:

- Abhi (Doctor)

Degree friends:

Geet (BBA), Punjabi girl.

This story is about Nidhi and how she leads her life beautifully. Since from her childhood she wants to lead her life as she wishes, she is like an open book; inside and outside, both are the same person. She has a lot of support from her parents and has a good group of friends. Allow me to introduce her friends gang, which is like her second family.

At school days:

Arpita, Arjun, Ajay, Ankit, Anusha, and Anjali.

1. Arjun: He was brought up under a single parent (father, owner of a company) and lost his mother at the age of four. He studied with Nidhi until the second later joined the engineering course. Nidhi means a lot to him; he adores her.

2. Anusha: She is also a wonderful, intelligent, innocent, and beautiful girl. She joined the doctor course. She always wants to be with Nidhi.

3. Arpita: She is also a friend of Nidhi; she joined the engineering course with Ajay.

4. Ajay: He is a very sweet person; after PU, he joined an engineering course.

5. Anjali and Ankit: Both joined BBA with Nidhi.

This is her school gang; in this group, Nidhi is like a leader, everyone's favourite. She is a loving girl; everyone wants to be with her because of her behavior and her kind nature. Every one of them is an expert in different things, like Nidhi and Arpita in dancing and Ankit in guitar.

In PU:

6. Abhi: a good-looking, dashing, intelligent boy with a little attitude-type boy.

Actually, their life started now after entering college. Competition, enjoyment, assignments, exams, ragging, everything ... But it teaches them a lot. So we will enter into their life of PU... a small description of their life before entering the degree level.

After finishing schooling, Nidhi started her tuition classes for small kids and started to earn for herself. As she is a very intelligent girl in school, a few parents joined their kids in her classes. With that earned money and her pocket money, she wants to donate some for orphans and old age homes. But still she is a first-rank student despite spending more time on other things.

On the first day of college, her gang entered the college; all her friends are intelligent students. On the first day, she met many new friends and also a special guy, Abhi. Abhi studied in that institution from primary, so he is very well known to everyone. Most handsome personality, very dashing and intelligent, but with a little attitude.

But Nidhi knows how to handle such types of boys. Classes started, and everyone was busy in their studies, with little masti and little competition, and that competition is between Abhi and Nidhi unknowingly. Nidhi's group became everyone's favourite. Everyone wants to be friends with Nidhi and Anusha.

In this beautiful journey, first-year results are out. As usual, Nidhi got first rank, and Abhi & Anusha got second place. Abhi felt sad and jealous; he took his studies very seriously this time, and this is his second year, so he started his studies as early as possible.

In the beginning of the second year, national-level competition is held in the college. College faculty planned for a drama of Krishna and

Radha. There are two groups in class, Nidhi's and Abhi's. Unfortunately, all are in drama. But the funny thing is Abhi is Krishna and Nidhi is Radha. Everyone is shocked after listening to the character's name. No one can imagine how they have rehearsed with such a big attitude issue.

One day Nidhi missed the rehearsal; Abhi was waiting for her for a very long time. The next day he came to know that she missed her rehearsal because of her performance at the marriage function. She earned some money from her performance and gave it to Orphan. He liked her simplicity, her hard work, and her selfless work. Slowly they became friends; unknowingly, Abhi got a crush on her. On the parallel side, Anusha has started to like Abhi…without his knowledge… Anusha has fallen in love with Abhi.

And one day Abhi proposed to Nidhi; she just refused and clearly said she treated him as just a good friend. He is a bit upset, but as time goes on, both forget everything and move on as good friends. But Abhi was in more touch with Anusha. In these days, Abhi and Anusha became good friends. Abhi understood that Nidhi was just a crush, not more than that.

One day Nidhi came to know that Anusha was in love with Abhi but didn't express her feelings. She noticed Abhi is more comfortable with Anusha than Nidhi. She went to Abhi and asked about Anusha; he said she is a very nice, intelligent, and beautiful girl. She asked whether you love her; Abhi said nothing like that, but I like her. She said, Then don't meet her for one week. After one week, Abhi came to Nidhi and said, I really miss her; I can't spend a day without speaking to her." Nidhi told him, "Pagal, yeh tho hai Ishq wala love." Abhi understood what he was talking about.

Finally, at last in PU, there are two couples in Nidhi's gang.

Abhi and Anusha

Arpita and Ajay

And a unique friendship started between Abhi and Nidhi. But he always wants to call Nidhi his Radha only, as she is his first crush. He loves Anusha more than himself. He knows singing, so he joined Nidhi's band set and started to help her in her work of donating to orphans. Whenever Nidhi calls him to perform, he will make sure to arrive on time in front of Nidhi. This is how their friendship story continues. He respects her a lot.

After the results, Anusha & Abhi got free seats in good medical colleges; Ajay, Arpita, and Arjun joined engineering; and Nidhi, Anjali, and Ankit joined BBA in Delhi. All are in Delhi only.

All their degree life started... In Delhi also, she started her charity work, visiting ashrams, vruddha ashrams, and hospitals. In ashrams, she is so attached to them so much that they don't want to begin their day without seeing her face. Before completing the first year of BBA, she is almost like a family member to them.

• In Degree:

Her life started from here; many changes occurred in her life. When she was in the second year of her degree, roadside she met a boy who lost his parents in an accident a few hours ago. He was crying, not knowing what to do; he stayed in a nearby slum. Nidhi felt very bad after listening to his story. She inquired about everything about him and thought to adopt him, but she faced much opposition from everyone—friends, parents, and even legal issues like the conditions and rules of law in adopting a child. The first time she used her papa's name to adopt, as legal documents say, she should have been financially strong. Finally, one day she completed everything and adopted a boy and became like Mother Teresa.

After all this, her life became full of hectic schedules, studies, ashram work, programs, taking care of a boy, tuitions, and everything she managed with a beautiful smile... She always maintains that smile.

In this busy schedule, she met a girl from Punjab, Geet, a very sweet and beautiful girl, and her presence makes Nidhi's group full of joy. Her Kannada mistakes many things…joyful girl.

One day suddenly everyone got the news that Arjun had met with an accident. Everyone is taking care of him shift-wise, as he is a single-parent kid. One day Nidhi came to visit him at his home. Everyone is busy with their work; only Nidhi came. His father went to his work and left Nidhi with a hospital boy-like nurse. The hospital boy went outside for some time. At that time Arjun wanted to go to the bathroom; it was very urgent to him. He waited for the ward boy to come, but he didn't, so Nidhi helped him to the bathroom, but he fell down there. Nidhi again helped him; with great difficulty, she brought him to the bed, but his clothes were completely wet. She waited again, but the boy didn't come. She tried his number; it's switched off, so she asked Arjun whether she could change his clothes. Obviously he refused. Nidhi is concerned about his health, that he may catch a cold, and his clothes are urinated on, so she told him one thing: "We don't know when they will come, so just think that I am not your friend; I am your mother. Please close your eyes; even I will." She started, but that boy came and helped her. She scolded him for not taking care of Arjun. Arjun started to cry… called her Yashoda, maa…. He said, "I don't know who will do this to a person other than a mother." I love you, and thank you for being with me in my life as my mother. His father came and asked for forgiveness from Nidhi for such circumstances. Nidhi said, "It's ok, Uncle. He is my best friend; he is like a brother." After this incident, Nidhi used to be called Yoshodha Maa by Arjun.

Nidhi wants to do many things, like secure that adopted child's life. One good thing about Nidhi is she is always ready to help others, whether they are strangers or people she knows. Nothing matters to her… she doesn't want to send anyone back who came to her for help. Sometimes this thing makes her friends worry about her, because she can be misused by anyone, so they always stood by her to protect her. Each and every one in her group will come to her when she needs them… such a beautiful and strong relationship she has with them.

One day she got late due to her programs. She wants to go to the NGO to meet her child; she got late. Her bus stop is a little far, so she has to walk by herself. She thought to call anyone to pick her up, but it's too late; she didn't want to disturb them. She thought to go alone, as we all know Delhi is not that safe a city. She is very strong, so she started her way to the bus stop. In the middle of the way, she got a call from her. Child, he asked, "wru?" She said, "On the way." He thought she was doing so many things for me. It's too late; she is coming alone. He came to the bus stop and waited for her. As she arrives, he hugs her and says, "I will come with you every time, wherever you go," and "Can I call you Mom?" Nidhi was shocked, and her eyes filled with tears, full of happiness and satisfaction.

The next morning their group meets for breakfast. In their conversation, they got to know that she came all alone to this unknown city, and that too from that long way. Everyone started scolding. Arjun took it very seriously. He stopped talking with her. At this time the ashram conducted an event. Nidhi invited everyone. She arranged many programs to entertain the people who stayed there. She and Arjun planned for a dance, but Arjun is angry with her; he went out with his girlfriend on the same day. Nidhi doesn't want to call him, as his GF doesn't like her. She waited for a long time; he didn't come, and she went off. One week went like this; still, he didn't speak with her.

One policy of her life is she wants to help others who are in need, whether they are misusing her or whatever else; still, she wants to help. She just thinks if she helps others, God will help her in her tough times. Weeks passed; he didn't speak with her. One day he was having an appointment with the doctor; every time, she used to join with him. But this time he didn't call her; he went with his GF. Before they reached there, Nidhi was already in the hospital with the required document in her hand. He is shocked; even his GF gets shocked and annoyed.

The doctor asked everything of Nidhi, not for his GF; it became indigestible for her. As they came out, Nidhi asked sorry for him. He didn't respond and started to walk away, but he came back and asked Nidhi, "Promise me, from now onwards, whenever you need help, you will call me, whatever the situation will be; you don't go alone anywhere." Nidhi smiled and hugged him and said sorry. They went home from the hospital with happy faces.

Finally, they finished the BBA. They decided to continue their studies further and want to join an MBA program. Anjali, Ankit, Geet, and Nidhi joined the MBA. Their new chapter of life started.

MBA:

Their life started, and many things changed once our new chapter started, but Nidhi is the same as before. Because of her kindness and politeness, she became a favourite student in the college, but drama in her life won't take a full stop. While she was going to college, she saw someone meet with an accident, and no one was helping the victims. She is Nidhi, so she went there and helped them get to the hospital using an auto driver's help. They went to the hospital where Anusha and Abhi are studying. But the receptionist told Nidhi that "we have to inform the police" and asked who she was and how she was related to that person. Nidhi thought if she told them she was like his relative, then they might treat them as early as possible, so she told them she was their daughter. After some time, they said they needed blood, and luckily Nidhi's blood matched that person, so she donated her blood. But Abhi and Anusha were tense because it was a police case, and she lied. How will she manage things if the police come and ask her?

When police came to the hospital and asked everything of Nidhi, she told them she lied because they were telling them, like, Until and unless there's a police inquiry, we can't treat him, so I lied to them that I am his daughter." Police were polite and understood the situation. They told her to come to the police station. Nidhi went with them, and Abhi and Arjun joined them.

After some time she finished her work, went to the hospital, met the patient, and informed their relatives. The patient came to know that because of Nidhi, he is alive. He called Nidhi near to him and said, "I don't have children, but you told them that you are my daughter. Thank you, kid.

God bless you. In the future, if you need any help, come to me at any time. And you are like my daughter only."

She used to go to the hospital every day to meet him, and she even met his wife also. Their relationship bonding became very strong day by day. After being discharged from the hospital, they maintained their relationship. They became so close that she started to call them Baba and Badi Ma. Life goes on with new relations in the world.

Everyone in her group is very proud of her and her decisions. They all respect her a lot. But Abhi always wants to flirt with Nidhi as his Radha.

On the other side, Arjun, Ajay, and Arpita finished their engineering and started their job searching. Arjun joined his father's company. Nidhi told Ajay and Arpita to join their company, which is in Bangalore.

Everyone started to settle in their life. On the other side, Arjun was planning to propose to his GF for marriage, but he was a little tense for his dad, so he asked Nidhi to convince his father. As his GF is a little modern and her father is a little egoistic. But because of Nidhi, he said yes, as he trusts Nidhi, and Nidhi trusts Arjun's choice.

Everyone is getting married, like Arjun, Geet, Ajay, and Arpita. But our Nidhi is still single. Someone will be waiting for her but doesn't know who that lucky guy is.

Arjun's engagement got fixed. But Arjun's father decided that Nidhi should take responsibility for the functions. Even his marriage customs should be handled by Nidhi only as his sister. So they went shopping. Arjun and his father wanted their daughter to take the first saree, as they don't have any daughters. They took a saree for Pooja and not for Nidhi. Arjun was helping Nidhi to select a saree. His GF got angry that no one was giving importance to her. She went off without saying anything. After some days his GF came to Nidhi and scolded her for coming in between them and warned that she should be their first priority, not you, so please stay away and maintain distance. Abhi heard everything as he came to meet Nidhi. As his GF went out after shouting. Abhi came inside and said to Nidhi that he would speak with Arjun. Nidhi stopped him and said, It's my fault that I went in between them, so don't spoil their function. While leaving, she also added that the saree that Arjun selected for Nidhi was liked by his GF first. Nidhi cried a lot.

On the day of the engagement, everyone is busy with arrangements for the function. Nidhi tried her best to avoid conversation with Arjun; she didn't even wear his saree. Purposely, she is avoiding entering the stage. Every time when he used to call her, she pretended like she had more work to handle. She can't miss the function, as she promised his father that she would handle everything. Arjun requested every one of his friends to bring her, but she somehow managed not to go there. Finally Arjun shouted her name and said, If she won't come now, I will come down from the stage to take her. She did not have any option to say no. Finally, she went there. Arjun asked her, "Why are you doing this?" She said nothing, yar. I was busy with work, and sorry I didn't wear the saree, as it has a blouse problem, so she stands for a photo. As soon as the photo was clicked, she came down. Arjun felt something had happened. After the function he asked her, and she said, "I was feeling a bit uneasy, a little feverish, so" and tried to stop the discussion there only.

After that, everyone became busy with their work. But Arjun is finding the reason behind Nidhi's behaviour. He felt Nidhi and Abhi were hiding something. So he went to Abhi and asked about the matter; basically, even Abhi avoided his questions, but Arjun tricked him by his words and found out the things that happened between his GF and Nidhi.

He went directly to Nidhi's home and asked her to forgive him for everything. He said, You are my best friend. I treat you like my mother, sister; you are family to me, my Yashoda maa. Without you, I can't imagine my life, yar. You held a special place in my life. How did you decide that you can't attend my marriage?" She consoles him and says, "Make a promise that you will not say a single word to her; she is right in her place."

After one week, Arjun kept a bachelor party, but he invited everyone, including his fiancé's family. At the party he requested everyone to share a few words about their beloved person in their life. Firstly, he asked Nidhi to speak. Nidhi came and started her speech. "I am Nidhi, and it's my family. I can't say I love this person more and this person less because everyone is equally important to me. I don't know what I mean to them, but I have a different relationship with them. Ajay treats me as his sister, Arjun as his Yashoda, Abhi as his Radhe, Arpita as his bhabi or as her sister Anusha as her southen, and Geet is my little baby. Ankit and Anjali are my best friends. They all are my family outside the house. They stood with me in my every situation. I don't want to say thank you because they deserve more than that." She started to cry, and everyone came on stage and hugged her. All the guests clapped at them.

Now others turn. Everyone came and took Nidhi's name, and they expressed their love for Nidhi and how she is important in their lives. Now it's Arjun's turn; he purposefully kept his last. He started his speech and told who his beloved person in his life was; except for his father, he took Nidhi's name and told the whole story of how he met her and how she became a friend to Yashoda, everything, because no one knew the story behind Yashoda, so he cleared everything and also told what Nidhi's place is in his life. He doesn't want to compare with anyone. At the same time his father joined him and said that no other girl wanted to do the thing that Nidhi did for us. She is my daughter. Love you, my kid. He said each and everything that a daughter will do in marriage, everything will be done by my Nidhi. Nidhi came and hugged Arjun and his father.

Arjun's GF came to know what she did; no one can do it as a girl. She understood that Nidhi's place is higher than hers in his life. She felt guilty with jealousy. She came to Nidhi and said, "Sorry, I came to know what you mean to them, but please don't take my place." But our Nidhi knows her limit. She smiled and left. His marriage is fixed for next year.

As the days passed away, Nidhi reached the MBA final year exams. She is still busy with her social work.

One day her parents called her and told her that "they are going to attend his close friend's anniversary function in Mumbai, and they told them to bring you also; you got a special invitation from them, so you have to come with us." She refused, but they ordered her, so she said yes. Her father's friend is a big person in a standard-wise way, even as a human being. A big businessperson in India has many companies in different sectors, basically belongs to Karnataka, and is currently staying in Mumbai. Nidhi decided to attend the function; she went to Mumbai with Ajay and Arpita, as they are workers at his pappa's company. All of them reached Mumbai at night, so they stayed in a hotel. In the morning, all of them went to their home for the function. Nidhi's father and his friends are childhood friends, so there will be more closeness, so only they were invited to their home.

{ This function will be the most memorable one in her life. She gets many new relations, and finally she will get her soulmate, as Nidhi decided not to marry, but she will fall in love... A new chapter begins in her life.

So our Nidhi entered the house with a beautiful white dress, the same as Pari's. She was in a simple white dress, but she was looking gorgeous and stunning because her inner positivity gave her an extra glow, and her peaceful smile made her more attractive. As she enters, each and every boy's attention is on her. They kept Pooja at home, and a big party will be at night.

Everyone was busy with their friends, including her father and mother. Ajay, Arpita, and Nidhi were standing in a corner. As Pooja got over it, Swami told her to do mangalaaarti and asked someone to sing a Pooja song. Her father's friend asked his son to sing, everyone shocked that a boy was singing an Arti song, everyone curious to see him. That boy started to sing. Nidhi was also shocked that he was singing so nicely. In the middle of the aarti, he coughed and stopped singing. Immediately, Nidhi started to sing the song. Once his cough stopped, she made a signal that he could continue the song.

But he is continuously watching Nidhi as he is impressed by her simple look and her voice. Love at first sight... After the Arti, he started to distribute Prasad for everyone. Nidhi came to know that he is the son of them; she liked his simplicity. His parents came to thank her as she helped during Pooja time. Her parents said it's okay; she knows that song, so she sang it. At the same time, Raj came to give Prasad something and to say thank you. Her parents introduced Nidhi to him, and his parents introduced his son, so finally Raj and Nidhi met.

After some time, everyone was busy with their work. Raj came to Nidhi, who was standing with her friends, once again thanked her, and started to discuss their education and all other things. After hearing about her college name, he asked why that college had any percentage issue. Immediately after his question, Ajay wanted to answer it, but Nidhi stopped him and told him why we have to explain. Later, they continued their talks. Rahim called Nidhi and told her that he got 1st rank. Nidhi got more excited, and with happiness she started to jump, hugging Ajay, and Arpita told her that Rahim got 1st rank.

But our hero Raj got confused why she was so happy and asked, Who is Rahim? She said, "My son," and he was totally shocked and asked, "Are you married? Ajay said, "No, no, she adopted a kid; his name is Rahim." Nidhi said, "I want to be with him, but we are here." Ajay asked her to call Rahim; he wants to talk with him. They decided to call Abhi and ask him to meet Rahim. Nidhi called Abhi and asked, "Where are you?"

He said, "In Rahim's party."

Nidhi got surprised and said, "Thank you."

He said, "Oo mere Jaan and mere Radha, I know why you called me. Don't worry, we are with him, and in fact, everyone is here with him."

Ajay told Nidhi that he wants to speak with Rahim. Abhi put it on speaker, and Ajay and Arpita congratulated Rahim. Everyone with Abhi asked for a treat for Ajay. Because Ajay challenged that if Rahim scored more than 75%, he would give him a treat. He said, "Ok, I will come to Delhi tomorrow, and we will do a party there."

Everyone on the other side of the call said, "Nooo."

Ajay said, "What happened?"

Nidhi said, "No, not tomorrow, as I am going to Bangalore, so…"

Ajay: "Why now?"

Nidhi: "I have some work."

Ajay, watching her expressions, got doubt. He asked, "Why suddenly?" Even Arpita also asked the same question. She said, "I have some personal issues, so I want to go there."

Ajay was serious and thought something might happen in Delhi, so she is going to Bangalore. She asked her, "Tell me what happened; otherwise, I will slap you if you hide anything from me."

He became too serious, so she thought to tell the truth as they were in function, so she was not having any option. She said, "Tomorrow Ajay and Arpita's engagement is there."

Everyone is shocked, more shocking to both as they don't know that their engagement party is there.

{I know all the readers could be shocked that the couples don't know about that. By the way, Ajay and Arpita's parents called Nidhi to confirm their relationship, and they are ready for their marriage, so the parents of both Ajay and Arpita met and decided to do the engagement, but Nidhi planned that it should be a surprise for them, so she and all her friends planned a surprise party for them without their knowledge. In fact, Nidhi only did all the shopping with her friends.}

Finally, Nidhi told Ajay and Arpita the truth and told them that she did all the shopping for them, including their engagement dress, and asked for forgiveness. Ajay said, I don't know when you all planned all these things; it's totally a surprise for me, but it's the best surprise in my life. Arpita also said the same thing. I don't know when my parents said yes and how they planned all these things, and about dresses, I don't have any problem that you selected it because I know your choice, so it will be great only.

In all these things, Raj was in shock and surprised. Nidhi explained everything to him. Abhi called and asked Nidhi what happened. Nidhi told him our surprise got revealed. Abhi reminds her that they have to buy the ring.

Raj congratulates them, and Ajay and Arpita invite him to their function. Even Nidhi invited him. Raj said, Definitely, I will attend but want to confirm with my father. His parents came there only to call him, but Ajay and Nidhi asked them for permission for Raj to attend their function. They said, Sure, why not? and congratulated them. Nidhi asked her parents if she could go to the market to buy rings. Raj's parents told Nidhi to go with Raj; he will show you the shops.

They all four went to the jewellery shop. They were busy selecting, but they didn't like any of them. Luckily, she met her Baba, whom she rescued in an accident. He told her, Come, I will show you another shop where you will get good varieties. They went to that shop, and they selected their ring and finalized that one. Her Baba selected a set of jumkis for her as a gift, but Nidhi rejected them and said they could gift them at her own function. Baba wants to buy a saree for his wife, so he asked for help from Nidhi. They went with them and selected a saree, and she only made the payment and said, This is a gift from her salary for aunty." He hugged her with tears and said, Love you, beta. Baba went to buy a dress for Nidhi at the same time. Ajay and Arpita also wanted to buy a dress for Nidhi as a gift. Both were selecting, but Nidhi and Raj were standing in a corner and watching them. Both came and said, Wear this. She said, I don't want any of these dresses. She told Baba you can gift me anything when it's my function, so wait till my day. He agreed. But Ajay and Arpita didn't. She said, Ok, I will take it, but I will take that dress, which was selected by both. Again they started to fight about whose dress was best. Finally, Nidhi signalled to Ajay that she agreed with Arpita, and they took that dress given to her.

After shopping, they went to a hotel. Baba was feeling uneasy, and Nidhi noticed. When Nidhi asked him about his tablet, he said it was in the car, but the car was in the parking slot, so she asked him about the kashaya, which his wife used to make him drink when he felt uneasy. He said, Yes, it will help me, but where can I get , Nidhi went to the hotel manager and met his main chef and requested to prepare the kashaya and shared the recipe. She asked the manager, What is the cost of using your kitchen? He said we don't charge for good things. Baba started to feel okay; Ajay bought the tablets from the car at that time. Raj was quite impressed by Nidhi and how she managed so easily without any stress.

Later Nidhi apologized for Raj, as she didn't buy the rings from his friend's shop.

Raj: "Hey, it's ok."

Raj asked, "Who is he?"

Nidhi said, "He is my uncle."

They went to Raj's home for the evening party. As soon as he arrived, he told them he met Nidhi's uncle there.

Raj's father asked Nidhi's papa, "You didn't tell me that his relative stays here."

Nidhi's father "I only don't know; just now I came to know."

Nidhi's father "We don't know how many fathers, mothers, sisters, or brothers she has outside the house. The only thing I know is we are her biological parents; she is my queen, yar."

Everyone laughed over there. After some time, Raj got a call from a band that used to perform at his evening party; they said they couldn't come as his band member got into an accident. Raj got worried and tried other bands for help at the last moment, but no one agreed. Nidhi noticed this and came to Raj, asked his problem, and said, I can make it." He asked, How? If you trust me, I can make your evening a night full of music, but you have to pay me. Her father came there, heard everything, and said, How can you ask him for payment?" Raj said, "Hey, it's ok, uncle, but the problem is she is my guest and owner of such a big company; it may affect your reputation in the party." He said, "Nothing like that; it's her passion and profession. I don't mind anything. In fact, I am very proud of her if she performs at my friend's party."

Nidhi: "Even if I don't have any problem, I am performing as a professional band, not as your guest, and paying for me is it. If you trust me, then give me a chance.

Raj: "Of course."

Nidhi: "But one request: make sure my band reaches the venue."

Finally the party started, and she is performing so well that everyone is enjoying it. Nidhi's father said to Raj's family that "she used to perform like this at parties and school functions and at marriages; of what they earn in that, she divides 50% to the band and 50% for herself, and again in that, she divides 25% to the orphanage and the remaining to Rahim's future."

Raj's father was impressed by her work. Lastly, Raj joined the band as he also can sing; later they danced to the music of the band. Even Raj planned to send some gifts to the orphanage people in the name of his parents, and Nidhi was impressed by him.

While having dinner, Raj's father praised Nidhi. Nidhi's father told them, She is like that only; in fact, you should meet her big gang, or do one thing: come to Bangalore tomorrow for Ajay's function, where you can meet her wonderful gang, and even we can meet our old friends."

Raj's father said, "Yes, it will be the best plan. We are planning for a trip, so it will be one."

They all decided to leave for Bangalore by night flight. They reached there at midnight, 12. As they landed, only one car was there. Another driver was on leave, so before leaving Mumbai, she called her Salman bhai to pick her up. She sent her parents with the first car. Arpita went with her brother. He asked Nidhi whether he should drop them. Nidhi said, "Don't worry, bhai, I arranged something already."

{ Before boarding the flight, Nidhi called her adopted granny and her maids to prepare her friends' favourite dishes, even Rahim's separately. }

Raj, Ajay, and Nidhi were waiting for Salman Bhai. Raj said, "We will go by taxi."

Nidhi: "No, my bhai will come."

Ajay: "Maybe he will be late."

Before finishing the sentence, her car came. She sat in the front seat, and both sat in the back. Salman Bhai gave her favourite dish. She was surprised and started to eat it, which was made by Salman Bhai's mom; later, she gave it to Raj and Ajay. Salman bhai said to Nidhi, "Come home to meet Mom after your function."

Nidhi: "Ok, Bhai, I will."

They dropped Ajay off at his home. They came to Nidhi's home. As soon as she entered, she called everyone, but no one picked up the phone. She asked Watchman Uncle whether they reached or not; he said "no" to her. Friends informed him that he should not say that they have reached her home, as they want to scare her. She, with tension entering the home, saw Orbit chocolate paper. She came to know that they had reached their destination but planned something, so she went to Watchman Uncle and asked once again. He said the truth, so she made the watchman ring the doorbell. Raj and Nidhi hide there only, and once they open the door, someone puts the water on the watchman instead of Nidhi.

Nidhi started to laugh and make them fall into their own trap and said sorry to the watchman that she didn't know they would pour water.

Watchman "It's ok, Putti, enjoy the day. I will change and come."

Nidhi "stupid"

Friends, "How did you get to know that we are here? Watchman Uncle informed you, na?"

Nidhi, by showing the rapper, "Arjun gave a hint by throwing his chocolate paper."

Everyone started to beat Arjun; he ran away as he is the one who eats the Orbit chocolate more often. Everyone welcomed Raj and Nidhi. Nidhi hugged her granny and her adopted grandparents.

{Adopted means both were working in their home for many years. One day their son left them in Ashrama. They stopped working in their house, so she adopted them and kept them with her, the same as Watchman Uncle, so she made both adopt Uncle as their son so all three live in the same house.

They arranged dinner for Raj and his family. She told them she had Salman Bhai's sweet, so she doesn't have anything. But her granny told her that she prepared jamun for her. Everyone was shocked that Granny didn't give them that; later everyone had that and went to sleep. The Nidhi gang is sleeping in the big hall, which is on the terrace, as it's their favourite place. Everyone went to sleep. They arranged a room for Raj, which is beside Nidhi's room.

Raj was busy in a call. Suddenly he saw that Nidhi was going somewhere. He followed her. She went to her parents and asked about their business, health, tablets, everything. Later, she went to her granny's room —same thing there—then to her adopted grandparents'—same thing there also. Next to the hall where everyone is sleeping, she kissed Rahim's head and corrected the blanket, and finally she came to her room, where Raj was standing, and asked, "What are you doing?"

Raj: "Following you."

Nidhi: "When I was in Delhi, they were all alone here. No one will be here to take care of them, so whenever I am here, I take full advantage of the time."

Nidhi: "Go and sleep now; it's already late."

The next morning, everyone got ready, even Raj. Nidhi planned to go with her friends, but Raj asked whether he could come with them. Nidhi told him, "It's ok; you can come with your parents, as you may get bored there."

Raj: "I can get bored here easily, so I want to come with you."

Nidhi: "Ok, then join us. Get in."

Some people went to Arpita's home, but Nidhi went to Ajay's home, as they don't want to do any work without Nidhi, as they are childhood friends. In fact, she has to do all the rituals as a daughter. His mother's favourite child is Nidhi. Ajay introduced Raj to his family. Raj was shocked to see what care Nidhi was getting from that family.

{ Blood relationships are not important to become a sister or daughter to anyone; any relationship in the world just needs a good heart and selfless love. }

Ajay's mom liked Raj. She came to Nidhi and told her to wear her new dress as the function might get started, and she went to get ready.

She came out with a new dress. "Uffff, she is amazingly beautiful."

Ajay's mom gave her new jewellery to wear. Everyone was so happy that they were all waiting for the girl to come.

They all came with Ajay's girl, Arpita. Ajay's mother called Nidhi to hold Arti's plate. As Arti was being done by Nidhi, Arpita's brother stopped Nidhi and said, In marriage, you should be on our side. Nidhi said, Ok, bro. The function started, and both families exchanged the dresses they bought for the couples. They went to the room to exchange them. Ajay was shocked to see that his dress colour was Arpita's favourite one, and Arpita's dress was Ajay's favourite one. She went to Arpita to help her get ready. Arpita hugged her and said, You are amazing." Ajay called Nidhi. Nidhi went to his room, and he hugged her and said, How do you think of these small things to make us happy?" Nidhi "stopped it, yar, anything for you, now come, it's time now." As they entered the stage, the gang was shocked that they were wearing their favourite color dress. They called Nidhi and said, "You are superb." Rituals started, and Ajay's father asked Nidhi to exchange the plates on their behalf.

After the function, everyone came in line and said, You are great, Nidhi, and praised her for her efforts in making this function so amazing. Nidhi was in a sentimental mood. Abhi noticed and said, "Oh, mere Radha, don't cry, please; otherwise, your Kajol will spread that you will look like a devil." Everyone started to laugh and all hugged, only Raj standing in a corner. Nidhi called him to join, and he felt very happy by joining their gang. Abhi started to flirt with Nidhi, and Raj got confused about whether they were in a relationship. Even he notices Anusha with Abhi. Later, Ajay tells him they are not in a relationship. He got confused and shocked about what the relationship was with her, and they respect her so much that even he started to respect her for her kindness and selfless love, which she is distributing everywhere.

After the function, Ajay's mother invited Raj and Nidhi's family for lunch. His mother called Nidhi's parents inside the room and told them that she liked Raj, even though his behavior is too good, so he is a perfect match for our daughter.

Nidhi's father: "Even I liked Raj; they make a good pair. Thank you for giving me this idea, but I don't know how to speak with his parents because he may misunderstand my words, or our friendship can get disturbed.

Raj's parents came inside and said, "It may get worse if you don't give your daughter to my son. In fact, I like your daughter. Before them, I thought about it even when I discussed it with my wife, and I came here because of this reason only. I thought to discuss this with you once I reached your home."

Raj's father "I want your daughter as my daughter-in-law. She is perfect for my home, and to my son, I know he might not be perfect, but trust me, she will make him perfect."

Ajay's mom and Nidhi's mom were full of happiness, but Nidhi's father said how we should convince them.

Ajay's mom suggested a plan: let them decide for each other whether they are made for each other or not; we will just make them come close.

Ajay's mom said, "Nidhi's father should go to Nidhi and should say, like, 'They like Raj; even they are searching for a girl, so I want him to be my son-in-law, only if she likes him. He has a plan for testing him. You can spend time with him and test him in your way. If you like him, then only I will speak with his father about marriage.' The same thing should be done by Raj's father to Raj: both should not know that already his parents agreed to the marriage and decided on marriage; in this way we make them close."

Nidhi's mother: "But Raj is going to London. How can we send Nidhi there, because we want them to spend time together?"

Nidhi's father said, "We will send her for some course in London as she is used to completing her MBA exams."

Everyone is happy that they got a good boy for Nidhi. The next morning everyone started to leave. Abhi, Nidhi, and Rahim stayed there only because Raj's father told him to stay here only for some project. Nidhi went to the hospital with her parents and granny for a regular checkup. Raj also went with them. As she went to the hospital, she told the doctor to check everything for all these 5 people. Nidhi went to donate the blood with Abhi's friend.

Abhi, watching Nidhi, said, "She always donates blood; she cares for everyone."

Raj: "Seriously, how can she think all these things? She is the owner of such a big company, but she is so simple and down to earth; she uses each second of her life."

Abhi: "Wait and watch what she will do; now she will bring fruits, chocolates, everything for patients."

Both went and watched her. Nidhi went to cancer patients and gave them Fruits chocolates and started to enjoy herself with them, as she had known them for a long time.

Raj asked Abhi, "How can she make everyone so happy so easily without any effort? Even she looks happy always. Has she been the same like this from the beginning?"

Abhi: "She is like a princess, yaar; she always takes care of things, she always cares for those who she loves, and, in fact, she helps unknown people also without any expectations. Once she starts to love them, she doesn't leave them in any condition; she understands everything just by watching them. Such a sensitive lady she is, strong and lovable, my Radha darling, yar. I got a new word for teasing her:

Raj laughed at him.

Nidhi came outside. "What are you doing here?"

Abhi: "I got a new word for you."

Nidhi: "Stupid, don't do any childish things here; it's a hospital."

She started to run.

Abhi, while following her, shouted, like, "My princess Radha darling."

Raj just smiled at them and at seeing their cute relationship.

After coming from the hospital, Nidhi went to her room. Abhi and Raj were sitting on the balcony, and they were watching all the photos in Abhi's phone. The next day, Abhi went back to Delhi. Nidhi and Raj roamed Bangalore the whole day.

At night Nidhi's father called her and said, "You told me once that you wanted to take a fashion design course, so I made your admission to the best center in London." Nidhi felt very happy, but at the same time she was upset that she had to go so far. At that, Raj came there and heard the things and said, "Oh, it's great-uncle. Even I will be there only so I can take care of her."

Nidhi's father said, "Thank you, my boy."

The next day, Raj went to Mumbai. Nidhi's father came to her to execute their plan.

Her father "I like Raj. If you like him, I can talk with his parents."

Nidhi "no"

Father: "Please, every one of your friends is settling except you. Please say yes. It's a known family. We will do one thing: as you both will be in London, you will roam with him, spend time with him, and if you feel he is perfect for you, then I will speak with his parents."

Nidhi "OK, only if I like him. In fact, both of us should say yes."

Other side in Mumbai Raj's father did the same thing, and even Raj said the same things. This is the second step in their plan.

{Finally, Nidhi's love story started. In everyone's life, couples first fall in love and then plan to convince their family, but here it's totally opposite: families loved each other, so they wanted to convince their children. }

After her exams, Nidhi started her planning to join her favourite course in London for one year. In fact, she decided to join Raj's company for a project that started between their parents, so on behalf of her father, she will be handling it there. She made Rahim's college admission in Bangalore with her parents. She kept a small party for all her friends. Everyone was happy that she was going to London. After that she went to London.

{To meet his Prince Charming}

Once she landed at the London airport, Raj was already waiting for her. She was surprised about his punctuality and happy that he welcomed her. As soon as she came out, her papa called her and asked, "Whether she got Raj or not." She said, "Yes, she met him; in fact, he is with me only." She gave the phone to Raj. Her father requested of her that she "please take care of her."

Raj: "Don't worry, uncle; from now onwards, she is my responsibility."

Nidhi smiled unknowingly; she didn't know the reason why she felt happy. Raj "Today, one night you can stay in my home because tomorrow you can join your college, only if you don't have any problems; otherwise, I will make smoother arrangements."

Nidhi went aside and called her father. "He is telling me to stay with him tonight."

Her father "I trust Raj; you can only feel comfortable."

Nidhi: "Even I trust him."

Nidhi "Raj I will stay with you today."

They both reached home, and there was a fat man waiting for them. Raj introduced him to Nidhi as his friend, caretaker, uncle, and everything. He arranged everything for her. While having dinner, Nidhi asked, "Whether my father told you that I am joining your company on a project."

Raj "Of course, in fact, I already arranged a cabin for you."

Nidhi: "No, I don't want any separate cabin for me. I don't want to work as a partner or daughter of a co-owner, because I want to learn so many things in this field, so I want to work as a common employee in your company; no one should know that I am a partner in this project."

He just smiled and said, "Maybe it's called simplicity and hunger for learning and dedication and respect for your work."

Raj: "Okay, done as your wish. I have one post. I will appoint you there with a salary."

The next morning she wakes and sees flowers with a beautiful message: "Good morning and welcome to London. All the best for your first day here. Have a nice day… Regards, Raj"

She smiled and called her father and said, "He is a good and nice guy."

{Somehow, the first approach is good. One thing that is very interesting about their story is that both are testing and trying to know each other and trying to impress each other, unknowingly planning for their future of staying with each other, which is quite interesting.}

She went to the office, and on her first day in the office, Raj introduced her to everyone as his father's friend's daughter. She will work here from now on and called some colleagues to help her. She is the first girl in the company to work from India; men were there, but others are foreign girls.

After this, Raj went to his cabin. A Punjabi guy came to Nidhi and said, "Oh ji, oh, finally an Indian kudi aayi gayi." He also said, "You are too beautiful, ji."

Nidhi smiled at him and said, "Thank you, ji."

Raj is watching everything from his cabin and is happy to see that she is enjoying herself with everyone without any ego or attitude, so much simplicity." He called his father and said, "Papa, she is really a nice girl."

After working hours they came home, and Nidhi started to pack her things to shift to the hostel. Raj said, "You can stay here only, na."

Nidhi: "I can, but I want to be in the hostel."

Raj: "Ok, your wish. Come, I will drop you."

Both went to the hostel; there, everyone, including the security guards, greets Raj. Nidhi was surprised by seeing that. Many girls said "Hi" to him from their room. The hostel warden came to Raj and hugged him. The warden started to ask everything of Raj. He introduced Nidhi as his friend, and as she joined the designing course here, she will stay in the hostel only and was told to take care of her.

Nidhi greets them and Raj to their friends, "Please take care of her; if anything happens to her, inform me first."

Nidhi smiled to herself and said, "Caring."

Warden "Don't worry, I will take care of her; moreover, she is Raj's friend, so everyone will take care of her."

Raj smiled at them and said to Nidhi, "If you need anything, please call me at any time; don't hesitate to ask anything, ok? Take care of yourself."

Nidhi: "Okay, I will take care of myself. You can go now and take some rest."

Raj greets everyone there and says, "Bye" to Nidhi and tells her to call him whenever she is free.

Nidhi enters her room, and as soon as she comes inside, everyone asks her, "Are you Raj's friend?" She is a little surprised and said, "Ha, I am his friend," and thought to herself that Raj has many girl fans over here.

At night Raj called and asked her, "Is she ok there? Does she want anything? If she is not comfortable there, she can come here."

Nidhi: "Nothing like that. I am alright here."

The next day she came to the office with a beautiful dress. Everyone said that she is looking very pretty, except a girl who is getting jealous of her as she is getting all the attention in the office. After office work she has to attend the evening classes, as she opted for evening classes at the university.

After the office work, Raj left the office first; later, Nidhi and other employees left. Nidhi decided to catch the taxi to reach the university. As soon as she came outside, she saw Raj waiting. Nidhi asked, "Why are you here?"

Raj: "Come, let's get into the car."

Nidhi: "Raj, I have class now; I have to reach the university within half an hour."

Raj: "So only saying that, get into the car; it's already late now."

Nidhi smiled and got into the car. Once they reached the college, Nidhi said, "Please don't do it again. I can manage myself. I want to be as independent as possible. If I need any help, I will call you directly. Please don't mind."

Raj: "Hey, it's ok; I can understand your point of view."

Raj: "Ok then, bye. Take care. See you in the office tomorrow."

Day by day it is becoming difficult to manage the things, but she is trying very hard. Day by day they are becoming close to each other. Raj understands the situation of Nidhi, so he called his employee, the one who is guiding Nidhi, and told them to give her less work, as she is a student, so she has to manage many things.

One day while returning to her hostel, a group of boys teased her. Somehow she managed to escape from there and reach the hostel. As soon as she entered the room, Arjun called and did the video call, as he does the video call daily to Nidhi to check whether she is ok or not. As he called, he saw she was tense. He asked, "What happened?"

Nidhi: "Nothing, I came by running."

Arjun asked again, "Tell me the truth, or I will come there immediately."

Nidhi told Arjun about what happened while coming back to the hostel.

Arjun: "Inform Raj, or I will come there."

Nidhi: "I want to tell him, but he will be busy with a lot of work, so I thought not to disturb him."

Arjun: "Ok, then I will come there today itself."

Nidhi: "Hey, it's ok. I will tell Raj."

Later, Nidhi forgot to call Raj. Arjun didn't want to take a risk, so he called Raj himself and told him everything and asked, "Did Nidhi inform you about this?" Raj said, "No, and thank you. At least you informed me. Don't worry, I will take care." Arjun got more angry now that she still hadn't informed Raj.

The next day again, while coming back, the same boys were standing there. As soon as they came near to her, Raj came there with the police, as he had been waiting there for the past half an hour just to arrest them red-handed. Nidhi was shocked to see him and felt a bit of relief. Police came to arrest them. Nidhi came there and asked the boys not to repeat this, saying, "I know your law is very strict, so once they file a complaint, then your future will be ruined. You all still look young, so please don't repeat it. I am Indian; I am a guest here. After reaching India, I want to say only one good thing about this country: please don't try to make your country shameful in front of others. It may happen to the same thing with your ladies also, so stop it and don't encourage it also."

Police said, "Thank you, girl; you are awesome and kind."

Nidhi: "Please leave them. I will not file a complaint."

Police "Boys, be grateful to her; next time I don't spare you, mind it."

Boys "Thank you, lady; we don't repeat it."

Nidhi: "You are like my brother, so don't say thank you."

They all went off, and Raj said in an angry mood, "Come, let's go." Nidhi got to know that he was angry at her. She just sat in the car. Once the car started, she started to say sorry.

Nidhi "I know I could have informed you; sorry for that, I just don't want to disturb you."

Raj stopped the car and said, "Now you are asking for sorry; you are my responsibility. If anything happens to you, what should I say to Uncle and all your friends? It's good that Arjun called me and told me everything. I think you just treat me as your company partner, not more than that."

Nidhi: "Hey, nothing like that. You are in my friend list; in fact, you are my good friend."

Nidhi held her ears and said, "Sorry."

Raj smiled at her and said, "Please don't repeat it again. Call me if anything happens. From now on, I will pick you up from the hostel."

Nidhi: "Okay, but tell me one thing: whether you told Arjun that I didn't inform you of anything."

Raj "ha"

Nidhi: "Definitely he will kill me."

Raj: "What? Who will kill you and why?"

Nidhi: "I told him that I will inform you; now he got to know that I lied to him, and he will scold me like hell."

Everyone at the conference asked about her; she said, Don't worry, guys, I am ok. She asked, "Where is Arjun?" Abhi told her, "He refused to join."

Nidhi got another call; she cut the call.

Raj: "Really, you guys fight? I want to see it."

Nidhi: "What do you want us to fight?"

Raj "No, but I saw you only enjoying teasing each other. I can't imagine your fighting so much."

Nidhi: "Today you will see."

Nidhi got a call again; it's Arjun's.

Arjun: "Where are you? , whether the problem is solved or not, whether you are with Raj, na."

Nidhi: "Ha, I am with Raj."

Arjun: "Ok, then do the video call once you reach the hostel."

Nidhi: "Ok, yar, I will, but sorry."

Arjun cut the call, Raj laughing at them.

Raj smiled at her and thought, How could she manage everything?" Pyaari hai yar.

They went to the restaurant for dinner. While having dinner, he asked, I want to listen to Arjun's scoldings.

Nidhi: "Once I reach the hostel, I will fulfill your wish."

Once they reached the hostel, she told Raj to stand a little farther away. If he sees you, then he won't scold me. Make him stand behind the camera and call Arjun. Arjun was scolded very badly. He noticed that she didn't wear the earphone, which means everyone can hear his scoldings. He asked, "Where is it?" She said, "It's in the room. It's ok. No one in this world understands your scolding except me.

Arjun started to laugh and asked, sorry for scolding her, "Please take help from Raj; otherwise, can I come there?"

Nidhi: "It's ok. I will call Raj when I need him."

She notices that he is not very happy. She asks him whether he and his GF fought. Arjun said yes; she told him to wait for 5 minutes, and she would call him back.

Raj: "What happened, and whom are you calling?"

Nidhi called his GF and asked whether they fought again. The GF thought to herself that if she said yes, then she would interfere in their matter, so she decided to lie and said, "No, but why do you ask this?"

Nidhi: "Arjun called me and was telling me that for my security, he will come here without you, so I thought you both fought again."

GF: "No, he is not coming. From here only he will arrange the things for you."

She cut the call.

Raj: "Why did you lie to her?"

Nidhi: "Wait and watch; she will call Arjun now and say sorry, and she will ask if he is going to London. He will say no, and then their patch-up will happen."

Raj: "How exactly do you say this?"

Nidhi: "I will call her again; her number will be busy. If she is speaking to Arjun, she won't receive my call. If I call Arjun, he will receive my call, so I will call her."

Nidhi called her, and her number was busy. Raj smiled at her. Arjun again called her and asked, "What did you do to her? She called me and asked, 'Sorry, can we patch up the things?'

Nidhi: "Your happiness is everything to me, so go and talk to her. Bye, take care."

Raj, smiling and looking at her, said to himself, "Actually, God created her in his free time with a lot of love, so only she is like that, such a selfless pagal girl."

Raj: "How did you do this?"

Nidhi: "You know she doesn't like me; she is very possessive about Arjun. She doesn't allow me to come in between them; she doesn't leave any chance for me to interfere in their life. She thinks that if she allows me in their life, I may take her place in Arjun's life. She doesn't know that she herself is Arjun's life; no one can snatch her from Arjun. In fact, Arjun himself can't do it, as he loves her more than anyone else, and she loves him very much, with little possessiveness. Of course, it should be there, na, as he is her boyfriend. He deserves more of his time than anyone else, so I use this weakness of hers to trick her," she laughed.

Raj also laughed and asked, "How can you take so easily that she doesn't like you? And she doesn't respect you; sometimes she hurts you."

Nidhi: "No, she doesn't hurt me; in fact, she makes me happier by showing lots of love to Arjun. By her small misbehaviour, things made me laugh; she is increasing my life span indirectly."

Raj was so deeply touched by her words and said, "Who you are, yar, you tolerate the things, forgive them within a second so easily, make everyone happy, live a simple life, and think everyone is related to us. "Sabko apna mana" is a very difficult thing, yar; hats off.

Nidhi: "Ok, ok, come, we will go. Tomorrow again we have to go to the office and say thank you."

Raj: "No, thanks, ok. From tomorrow I will pick you up from college.

Day by day their friendship deepened, and they started to have feelings for each other, but not getting what it is, becoming close to each other. One day, a small party is organized. Before coming to the party, Raj asked Nidhi, Can you join with me for a dance?" She said, "Yes." Everyone was in a party mood, and everyone was looking good, but Raj and Nidhi were looking extraordinary. Everyone's eyes were on Nidhi as she was looking very beautiful. Everyone wanted to dance with Nidhi and Raj. All the boys started to ask Nidhi for a dance, and as she politely danced with everyone, Raj felt a bit jealous. He also didn't know why he was feeling like she belonged to him and not anyone else in this world; she is his girl. She said before that she would dance with him, but now she is dancing with everyone except Raj. Feeling bad and standing aside with a sad face, Nidhi noticed that she felt guilty, so she also decided not to dance with anyone, later messaging him and saying, Let's dance. He felt happy and thought that he had some space in her life.

They danced so well that everyone was shouting and cheering them, as they both trained in salsa, but one girl got upset and acted like she fell down. Raj and all noticed this and went to help her. Raj is a boss, so he took extra care. Somewhere Nidhi got upset that he went there without caring about her; actually, he went there just to help her; he went to drop her off. Nidhi felt bad that he didn't think about her.

After dropping her off, he started to move towards home but suddenly realized that he left Nidhi there alone. How will she go now? He tried to call her, but she didn't receive it. Finally she received .

Raj: "Sorry, yaar."

Nidhi: "I told you I would drop you, but the situation became such that I forgot and left you there only. I'm really sorry."

Nidhi: "It's ok, I can understand."

Nidhi: "By the way, you danced very well today."

Raj: "In fact, I should thank you for giving me your time to dance with me in your busy schedule."

Nidhi: "What? Busy na."

Raj: "Ha, everyone wants to dance with you today."

Nidhi: "If you had approached me before them, I could have danced with you first, but you were busy with your employees."

Both started to laugh at the same time.

{ Pyaar tho yahi se shuru hota hain na, jalan jagada aur hak se hi shuru hota hai. }

Daily their routine is to call their fathers and inform them of what they did and how they are feeling; their father got confirmation that they will fall in love as soon as possible.

They were feeling very secure with each other; they are very happy with each other. In her university they arranged a fashion show as their assignment, Nidhi designed many dresses and her friends are her models, she choose one of her friend to be her partner and they decided to wear Indian tradition dress, she is wearing saree and other boy who is her good friend of her wore Indian attire designed by Nidhi, Raj also invited there, he heard the rumour that Nidhi and that couple might be couples, so only she choose him over other handsome boys, he felt bad, but as the show started , before her turn her partner fell down and his leg got fractured , she was in tension , raj went to her and said what happened , she explained everything to him and his help , Raj said no way I cant do that. Nidhi pleased him; finally, he said yes.

Their turn came, and Nidhi and Raj went to the stage. Everyone is shocked to see them. They are looking good as a pair. After her ramp walk, she took the stage to thank everyone out there, including Raj, who helped her at the last moment. She clarified that boy is not her boyfriend; they are just friends. Raj felt very happy. As the show got over, Raj went to his home. He called her, but she didn't pick up the call. Many times he tried but didn't get a response. He got angry. After some time she called him and said she was in the hospital; she needed his help, so please come as soon as possible. He ran away to the hospital. When he saw her, he felt relaxed and started to scold her: "Why didn't she pick up the call? You know how much I get tense if anything happens to you. Then what about me? What should I do?" Suddenly he stopped there only and the moment he realized that he loved her so much.

Nidhi: "Stop it now. I need your blood. Please donate your blood."

Raj: "What?"

Nidhi: "While coming back to the hostel, my friends met with an accident, so I came here with her. They told me they need blood, so I called you."

Raj went and donated the blood. Raj was smiling continuously. At that time Nidhi didn't understand what he said, but he understood what he felt for her.

Nidhi: "Sorry, I made you worry. Drink this juice."

Raj: "It's ok, come, we will go home."

Nidhi, while going, started to explain everything to him, but he just smiled, looking at her, full of love. He dropped her off at her hostel; after that, he parked his car inside and started to dance and called her parents and informed them that he was in love. They were very happy, as they liked Nidhi very much. Raj wants to propose to her but wants to make it a more special day for her, so he thought to do it on her birthday.

The next morning, in the office, as Raj enters, everyone is watching him because of his extra glow on his face. He looks like he is the happiest person in the world; he used to stare at Nidhi. Raj wants to know what Nidhi feels for him. But they were getting close to each other day by day. One evening Raj, Nidhi, and that girl were there in the office. All three have some work, so they are staying. They went to have tea. The girl was already feeling insecure because of Nidhi, so she planned to propose to him, as only they were there. She told Nidhi to go outside as she had to speak with him alone. Nidhi came out feeling a little upset that Raj was with another girl, and that too alone, and he didn't say to stay back in the room. She proposed, but Raj said, I am already in love with someone, so please be a friend and a good colleague." She is a very mature one and said, Ok, but if you want to change your mind, please reconsider my proposal. She went off with tears in her eyes. Raj came outside and told Nidhi about that.

Nidhi: "What did you say?"

Raj: "She is just my employee, that's it."

Nidhi smiled at him; he understood it a bit but wanted to confirm it from her side. One day he didn't come to the office as he was having a fever. He didn't inform Nidhi, and as Nidhi came to the office and noticed he didn't come, she called Raj and asked what happened. Raj said he had a little fever, so tomorrow he will come and meet you. Nidhi went directly to his home, greeted his chef, and went to his room, feeling sad that he was not well. Raj: "Nothing to worry about; he took tablets."

Nidhi: "Oh my god, you have a high fever by seeing his temperature. Come, we will go to the hospital."

Raj: "I took a tablet, don't worry."

Nidhi: "We should not neglect this."

Raj and Nidhi both went to the hospital. He went to OPD as she stayed back to fill in the details. The doctor suggested they stay there for one night so that they could give him drips, as his fever was high; they agreed.

Raj: "You go to the hostel; Uncle will come to me or my PA."

Nidhi: "No need to call others; I am here, na."

Raj: "Don't worry, I can manage."

Nidhi: "It's decided that I will stay here."

Raj smiled and said yes, she made him eat food and helped him to go to the washroom. They came close to each other, and Raj understood that even she has feelings for him, while the discharging nurse asked Nidhi whether they were a couple or living in a relationship.

Nidhi: "No."

Nurse: "Sorry, but you were taking care of him so nicely that I felt like that."

Nidhi: "We are friends, my good friend."

Nurse: "Ok, take care."

Nidhi, thinking to herself that he is more than that, called his father and explained everything. Father: "Whether he is a friend like others or something special."

Nidhi: "No, I feel differently for him, not like Arjun and Abhi."

Father: "Then find out what that is."

Nidhi: "Maybe I started to like him, maybe in love."

Father: "Exactly what I was trying to explain to you."

Nidhi: "Okay, Dad, he came. Leaving for home now."

Raj and Nidhi went to their home. She stayed there late at night and later went to the hostel. While going, she was thinking about Raj only. Finally, she realized that she is in love with Raj. At night she called all her friends and put them on conference and told them, "I am in love."

All: "Come again."

Nidhi: "I am in love."

All: "Who is that lucky fellow?"

Nidhi: "You all know him."

Arjun: "Raj."

Nidhi: "Ha, how did you come to know that?"

Arjun: "I know your choice; he is perfect for you."

All: "Congratulations, we want to meet you now and want to do a party."

All, "Really, he is perfect for you."

Nidhi: "Wait a minute, but I don't know what he feels for me."

Arjun: "Ok, I will ask him."

Nidhi: "No, I will ask him."

All: "Don't worry, he will say yes definitely."

Nidhi: "Hope so far, feeling a bit nervous."

All: "When did these happen?"

Nidhi "don't know"

We will be waiting for good news.

The next day, both went to the office. She got ready just to impress him; she wants to spend time with him every time, and Raj also feels the same. Both planned to express their feelings on Nidhi's birthday only. Till date they were enjoying each and every moment with each other without knowing each other's feelings.

Finally that special date came. Everyone was excited to hear her good news. Raj planned a surprise party for her, and both are confident that both may say yes. Both decided to propose at the party; she came to know that he organized a party for her. But their parents didn't discuss with each other that their kids loved each other; they thought to surprise each other and discuss it when they met.

Raj called Nidhi, "Where are you?"

Nidhi: "2 minutes."

Raj came outside to welcome her by holding her hand.

Nidhi's car, just to enter the gate, met with a big accident.

Raj shouted, Nidhi!" Everyone was shocked to see the accident, as everyone believed that Nidhi died on the spot. Raj went there and grabbed Nidhi and went to the hospital without a second delay; as soon as they entered, the doctor went to the emergency room. Even the doctor thought she might not be as she is in serious condition. Everyone tried to call her to know what happened, as she has to propose to Raj, but her cell is not reachable. Everyone was tense, so they thought to call Raj only, as. He picked up the call and told everything. Each and every one started their journey towards London; in fact, her adopted baa and mommy decided to come. The doctor came outside and told them, "We can't say anything now. only." After some time, she got a little consciousness. She heard that doctor saying that they have to remove her uterus, as it got badly damaged and was bleeding continuously. She signed something for them. Doctor, don't make stress. I will speak to your parents, Nidhi. No, please do your procedure. I want to leave with him happy ever after; please save me. At that time everyone came to the hospital and started to cry to see Nidhi. Even Raj's parents came and hugged Raj. Raj said, "Pappa, see what happened to Nidhi. I want to propose to her, but my fate is too bad, Papa. I want her; I need her. She is the only girl in my life who I love most; she is my life." Everyone who heard that felt happy that he loves her.

Inside the OT, the doctor told them that they had to make them sign the consent form. Nidhi told them to call her father inside alone. They called her father and said what she told them. He agreed and said that he doesn't tell anything outside; please save my daughter. They started their operation, succeeded, came outside, and said she was out of danger, but she needed to regain consciousness after 24 hours. After seeing her condition, we will decide next. After 24 hours she shifted to the ward; her parents went to meet her, and later her friends. Everyone said that they were missing her.

Abhi: "Pagal, you can't go alone, without us."

Arjun: "You are here because of me, not because you are a good person."

Everyone was crying. Nidhi: "Signed, Don't Cry."

Nidhi is searching Raj, Arjun: "We know whom you are searching for, Raj, na. I will send him; in fact, I told him to go, but he refused."

Nidhi: "You are my priority; don't tell him anything."

Arjun sent Raj inside. He wanted to hug her but controlled himself and asked, "Why do you want to go alone? Don't dare to do that."

Nidhi: "No, I don't want to go alone anywhere."

Raj asked about her health; the nurse told him to go out. As the day passed, she started to recover. Everyone went back to India except Arjun, who stayed back there with Nidhi's parents, Raj taking care of her more than her parents, not allowing anyone to take care of her. By seeing this, Nidhi thought to tell him everything because she thought time is not permanent for anyone. One day Raj took Nidhi to the garden area in a wheelchair. There, she thought to tell him about her feelings. He started to play with kids there, and Nidhi asked, "You love kids?"

Raj: "I love them more. I feel very happy when I am with them. You know I already planned many things for my future kids; don't laugh, ok? As I'm thinking all these things without marriage, I love them more than anything in this world."

Nidhi stopped herself from expressing her feelings. They came back to the hospital. Raj went to the office for some meeting. Nidhi told her parents and Arjun what the doctor said to her in the OT, so she can't give birth. Her mother started to cry like hell, as only a woman knows how it feels when she can't give birth. Her father said, I will speak with his parents and will tell them everything; they will decide what to do next.

Arjun: "Don't worry, Uncle, they will say yes. I know Raj loves her more than anything else.

Nidhi: "Stop, don't call them. I don't want to marry him."

Arjun: "Why?"

Nidhi: "I don't want to ruin his happiness."

Arjun: "Stupid. In whatever time you are, love matters the most. Raj is an understandable guy; he doesn't step back."

Nidhi: "I know he won't step back as he loves more, but he loves kids equally. He dreamt of having kids now only. He planned so many things for them. He is the only son to their parents; they will say yes because of their friendship and because of Raj, but I don't want to be their daughter-in-law. I am not that lucky, yaar. After knowing his dreams, I don't want to ruin them."

Arjun: "Don't be stupid; you love him, and he loves you. How can you take his happiness from him? He can't live without you."

Nidhi: "Still, he doesn't know that I love him, so it will be easy to move away from him, a little difficult for him, but he will manage it."

Arjun: "What about you? You were waiting to see him on accident day. How can you stay without him your whole life?"

Nidhi: "I don't know anything. I have to stay; you all will be there, so it will be easy.

Her father said, "Ok, it's your decision, your wish."

After Nidhi's recovery, Raj's parents asked about marriage planning. Nidhi's father said, "Our plan failed. She is not in love with Raj. Sorry we couldn't make it; she might not be lucky enough to become your daughter-in-law."

His father came to Raj and said all the things. He was shocked to hear it and said, This is not correct. He thought even she felt the same and decided to meet her personally. He came to the hospital.

Nidhi: "Hi, Raj, come inside." started to talk casually, Raj got irritated and asked, "Will you marry me?"

Nidhi: "What?"

Raj: "Will you marry me?"

Nidhi: "Sorry, I am not interested in marriage. Even if I didn't feel anything with you, I didn't see you like that. You are my friend, in fact, my best friend. That's it. I am sorry if any of my moves made you feel like that. I didn't say I love you any time.

Raj wanted to say something but went off without saying anything. As he went outside, she started to cry. He went home and went to his room and locked himself inside; both are remembering each other and crying.

As days passed away, she recovered 70%. She called Raj and said, She can't go to the office as she is in the last term of her course."

. Raj said, "Don't lie; I know why you don't want to come. As you said, we are friends, so as a friend, come to the office. I am sorry for what happened in the hospital. The project is also in its last stage; it will end soon, so please come."

Nidhi: "Ok, I will inform Pappa and come."

Nidhi: "Pappa, I got some other time to spend with him. So I want to go without missing a day."

Nidhi started to go to the office, and they both maintained a little distance. They both are enjoying their journey as colleagues and good friends. When she needs help, he will come without any delay. She is not fully recovered. One day her car didn't come, and Raj asked her to get into the car.

Nidhi: "No thanks, her driver will come."

Raj: "Please, come inside. You can't stand for more time. If you think I am your friend, then come in."

Nidhi got into the car and said, "Don't use those words again; you will always be my friend."

Raj: "Because of the past, I don't want to lose this friend; you are a very special friend to me."

Nidhi: "Me too."

After that, they are moving each other as friends. Within a short period of time, they enjoyed a lot as friends. Both are full of emotions, but they don't want to express them. They think that these moments will be the wonderful moments of their lives.

After her course completion, she wants to move back to India and doesn't want to be in touch with him. Until her presence in his life, he can't move on, so it's better to keep distance from him." She said, Raj, that she will go back to India after her completion. Raj decided that he would keep a sendoff party for her in their office.

Raj told everyone that "Nidhi is not just an employee; she is my business partner, the daughter of our partner and co-owner. She wants to learn the things from basic, so she joined as an employee."

Nidhi, seeing their colleagues faces, smiled. "Hey guys, don't worry, I don't share your secrets with Raj; they will be our secrets. I don't want to tell anything about gossips; in fact, I will try to solve your problems by discussing them with Raj."

Everyone smiled at her and said, "We will miss you."

Nidhi: "Even I will miss you guys."

Everyone danced and had fun and even requested Raj and Nidhi to dance; they danced. They sent her with beautiful memories.

The next morning she went to India with a heavy heart, as she was leaving her love of life there only, but with beautiful memories. She reached India and went to Bangalore, later joining her father's company. Whenever Raj called her, she tried to avoid him. Raj understood that she was not interested in him now, so he stopped calling. As their project was over, they kept only a professional relationship, and that too most of the time it should be with their parents.

After some time she decided to shift to Malaysia. They started many branches over the world, one in Malaysia, which she wants to handle. She moved there with Rahim. Only she and her son shifted; her friends all stayed in India, but she is in touch with them except Raj.

As the days passed, one year passed away. Within one year, many things changed. Ajay and Arpita got married, and even Arjun decided to get married next year. She just went to Ajay's marriage, attended it, and came back to Malaysia. Even Raj was invited, but he missed it because of some office schedule.

After some time, Arjun went to Malaysia to meet Nidhi. They both had more fun, and their talks didn't stop. In between, he asked, "Are you happy?"

Nidhi: "Ha, I am."

Arjun: "My marriage got fixed this year-end. You should come one month before, as you promised that you would handle all the rituals. I need your help; even Pappa became a weak little thing, so I need your help as I'm alone."

Nidhi: "How can I come there a month before?"

Arjun: "I know you want to stay here only, but please, except for you, I can't ask anyone's help."

Nidhi: "Okay, I will come."

Arjun "I am inviting Raj also."

Nidhi: "Your wish, I don't have a problem."

Arjun went back to India, and after some days, she is getting ready to go back to India to attend the marriage, as its date is near. She decided to go with Rahim. On the other side, Raj planned for the India trip as he had some business meetings there. He decided to fly to India on the same day. Destiny has better plans for them. Both arrived at the airport at the same time. But he didn't inform Arjun; he wanted to give them a surprise.

Arjun and Ajay were waiting for Nidhi at the airport, but Raj came out first. He saw Arjun there and came to him.

Arjun: "Oh, you are here. You didn't inform me that you are coming."

Raj: "I want to give a surprise, as I am having some meetings here, but because of my bad luck, everything got flopped."

Raj: "By the way, who are you waiting for?"

Ajay: "Nidhi."

Raj is shocked and surprised; even he is happy that he can see Nidhi after almost two years.

Arjun: "Oh, there she is coming."

As Nidhi arrived, both Arjun and Ajay went to her; Raj stood there only just watching her and having a big happy face. Nidhi, shocked to see Raj there, thought to act normally. Even she acted normally as a business partner, just spoke formally, and even Raj spoke with Rahim.

Raj: "Oh guys, it's time to go now."

Arjun: "Where are you staying?"

Raj: "In hotel."

Arjun: "How can you stay in a hotel? Your friends are here."

Raj: "It's ok. I will come home once to meet Uncle, but now I will stay in the hotel."

Nidhi's father came to pick her up. Raj greeted her father, heard all the discussion there, and said, If your father comes to know that you are staying at a hotel, then he will kill me, so it's my order that you will stay in my home till you stay in Bangalore."

Raj, seeing Nidhi's face, said, "Uncle, I will speak with Father; don't worry, I will stay in the hotel itself."

By seeing Raj's face, "he told them that he didn't need to stay there; he would stay in my home. Uncle, please don't force him."

Raj finally agreed to stay in Arjun's home. They all said bye to each other and went to the car.

As Raj entered his home, he saw Nidhi and her friends picture. He smiled at it; Arjun noticed it. Nidhi wants to go to Arjun's home but is feeling anxious about how to face Raj there. Rahim says, "Don't worry, Ridhima, we will manage," as he knows she still loves him.

As Nidhi entered Arjun's home, Raj came to know that she was here; he came down, and Arjun noticed this also, and even Rahim. But Nidhi went to the kitchen to see the things and arrangements. She started to keep herself busy in marriage works. Raj was going to the office before leaving the house; he just saw Nidhi and went off. At night Nidhi went to her home. After dinner Arjun and Raj were spending quality time while chit-chatting. Arjun asked Raj,

Arjun: "When is your marriage?"

Raj: "Not yet decided."

Arjun: "Whether you selected any girl."

Raj: "No, yaar, I haven't selected any girl till now."

Arjun: "You are still single."

Raj: "Ha, it may remain the same in the future also."

Arjun: "What?"

Raj wanted to divert his topic, so he said, I am feeling sleepy, yar, so good night, and started to go to the room. Arjun stopped him and asked, "Do you still love Nidhi?"

Raj didn't answer.

Arjun asked, "You don't want to marry?" Again, Raj didn't answer.

Arjun: "Tell me, damn it, whether you still love Nidhi."

Raj: "Ha, I still love her, and I will be loving her in the future also. I can't imagine anyone in her place."

Arjun: "Nidhi doesn't love you; you should think about your parents."

Raj: "I thought about them, so only I said yes to meeting a few girls, but I didn't like anyone, so I rejected them. In fact, my parents also rejected them; they compared each girl with Nidhi, and no one matched their expectation. Nidhi's impact is more on them than on me, but we all tried to move on. In some cases they tried to convince me, but they couldn't, so they decided to leave me as I am."

Arjun, shocked to hear all those things, thought about how much they love Nidhi, she thinking she is not in their life, but they are leading their life with Nidhi's memories. Suddenly he thought he should inform Nidhi about this and have to make something for them. They can't be like this. What should I do? I can't do anything.

Raj: "Arjun, please don't say anything to Nidhi."

He said good night and went to sleep. The next morning, Nidhi came to Arjun's home. Arjun wanted to tell her something, but Raj stopped him. He told them today he is going back to London and will join them at their wedding. Arjun said, "Please don't go, as marriage is near only."

Raj: "Don't worry, I will come."

Raj said bye to everyone and went off.

For the marriage, Raj's parents also invited their business friends. Arjun and Nidhi did their shopping. Arjun gifted her a jumki of his mother's. Nidhi said, "I don't want to take it, as it should belong to his wife."

His father said, "You are like my daughter, and you took care of Arjun as his sister, mother, and good friend. You are handling all the rituals of our house, so basically it belongs to you. Don't reject them."

Arjun: "Because of you, everything is happening. Other jewellery all belongs to my wife, but this is my mother's, so I want to give it to you."

Nidhi smiled with tears and said, "Ok, but why do you both love me this much? I don't deserve all this."

Arjun: "Don't repeat it again. If you think you don't deserve us, then go to your home."

Nidhi: "Sorry." She hugged him and made him smile.

At the same time, all their friends came and said, Smile now only because after this you can't smile because of wives. All came and met Nidhi, started to chit-chat and pull each other's leg, and they started their work for marriage. Home is full of laughter, happiness, and masti. Arjun called Raj and asked him to come.

Finally, the marriage day has come. Arjun's father gave bangles to Nidhi and told her to give them to the bride. As she entered the room, Arjun stood outside the room without their knowledge to watch them, as he is worried that his GF may hurt her again, but she stood up as she saw Nidhi, gave more respect, hugged her, and asked, "How are you?" Nidhi felt happy that she was asking that instead of her harsh words. Nidhi gave bangles to her and said, "These belong to your mother-in-law. I am just giving it to you instead of your father-in-law. You are the luckiest one, as you got Arjun as your husband and Uncle as your father-in-law, and sorry if I crossed any line. I know that you don't like my interference in your life, but I am helpless in front of their love for me, so I came here and arranged everything. If you don't like anything of mine, please forgive me."

GF: "What about these jhumkas?"

Nidhi: "Arjun gave me these to wear. These are Aunty's. Ohh, sorry, I know these belong to you. I told them, but they forced me to wear these. I will return them tomorrow. If you want it now, I will give it to you, as they match your saree."

Nidhi started to remove them, but she stopped and said, "Please forgive me. What I did with you is totally wrong. I thought you were taking my place. Because of insecurity, I did all those things, but I know that you already have such a special place in their life. I came to know that if I remove you from their life, they can't be happy. I did everything to separate you from him after knowing how you saved him. Still, I did it. You both tolerated every misbehaviour of mine. Sorry, you arranged everything as his mother's sister so nicely. I like every bit of it. About these jhumkas, you deserve more than this. In fact, I respect you a lot and started to love you, yar," hugged Nidhi. Nidhi cried and said, "Thank you for understanding me, and this sentimental face doesn't suit you."

Arjun came inside and said, "Love you both." GF said, "So you were standing outside and hearing our conversation? You have doubts that I may hurt her again." Arjun said, "No doubt I know you so only standing out." Arjun held her hand and said, "You both are two eyes of mine; if one eye gets hurt, I feel restless and can't control the pain, so take care of each other."

All three hugged, and Nidhi gave his hand to her and said, "It's your responsibility now." She said, "Arre yar, we can't do anything without you; we still expect you to handle everything, so your whole life you will be taking our responsibility."

Nidhi cried and said, "Come, it's time to go now." She brought them to the stage. At the time Raj came there with his parents, he started to see her as she was looking very gorgeous in traditional attire. But Raj's parents want him to meet their friend's daughter. They made him meet her and left them to talk. Nidhi got to know that from Arjun's father. She felt a little bad. Her friend came and said, "We will go to some other side."

Nidhi: "It's ok; I am happy that he is trying to move on." She went off, and her friends started to sing a song that is practiced for Arjun's function. They started it a bit early just to divert her mind. Nidhi also joined them. Arpita and Nidhi planned for a dance; they started it in between their song. Everyone was cheering them, and Arjun from the stage said, "You all made my day, guys." Everyone was clapping for them; Raj couldn't resist dancing as he is also a dancer. All of them danced and enjoyed themselves and made a special for Arjun. Raj felt happier by seeing Nidhi's happiness. Everyone felt that Raj and Nidhi were made for each other.

After marriage everyone went to their places and started getting busy in their lives. Nidhi is back in Malaysia. After 6-7 months, Arjun went to London on business. Arjun called Raj and said, I am coming to London; we will meet there. Raj was told, in fact ordered, to stay in his home. Arjun stayed in Raj's place. After two days he noticed there was a room that was locked, but only Raj could go there. He asked him about that as he was very curious to know about the room. Raj refused to share. Arjun forced him, Raj, to take him to that room. As they entered, he was shocked to see it, as the room is full of Nidhi's photos; he thought he madly loved Nidhi. He felt like he should tell everything but stopped himself from saying it. He just went to his room with a heavy heart.

The next morning Raj told me that he is going to the hospital as someone needs his blood, so I am going. If you want to join me, you can. Both went to the hospital. As they reached there, Raj said, "This is the hospital where she made me donate the blood forcefully; this is the hospital where she rejected me."

Arjun was shocked and went to donate the blood. In fact, Arjun donated the blood to the blood bank. After the donation, they were sitting outside having juice. A doctor came to them and asked, How is Nidhi?" She was the one who treated Nidhi. Arjun, who recognized her, replied to her and said she was fine now.

Doctor: "She is not in contact with me after moving to Malaysia."

Arjun: "She is busy in some of her projects, so."

Doctor: "Really, I didn't meet any girl like her; none of my patients are like her. Such a strong willpower she has. In such a critical condition and in an unconscious stage, she was saying, like, she wanted to live, she wanted to spend her whole life with him, so please save me."

Raj was shocked by her words in OT. Asked the doctor, "Him? Who is that?"

Doctor: "I don't know, but she loves him very much, but her guts—uff, she is a very strong girl. As we told her that we have to remove her uterus, within a second she said, Ok, she just wants to lead her life with him happily."

Arjun tried to stop her, but she didn't stop, and after telling everything, she went off. Even Arjun said, "I have some meetings; I will go now." On the other side, Raj, without listening to Arjun, just thought to himself about what all happened in the OT and how she controlled herself, that, as she can't give birth, how could she feel that? He started to feel very bad for her. Arjun stopped his overthinking and said, "I want to see the bridge; we will go there now."

Raj is confused about who that person is whom Nidhi loves very much and why she didn't tell us. They went to the bridge, and Raj finally asked him, "Who is that guy?"

Arjun: "I don't know."

Raj: "If she loves him that much, then why is she not with him?"

Arjun: "I don't know anything."

Raj: "Why did she hide that operation from me?"

Arjun didn't answer anything and kept quiet. Raj, by seeing his silence, came to know that Arjun was knowing everything, so he forced him to tell everything.

Arjun finally opened up and said, "It's you whom she loves most in the world, in fact, still loving unconditionally."

Raj was shocked, surprised, and happy. and asked, "OK, if what you are telling me is the truth, then why did she reject my proposal?"

Arjun: "It's true that she loves you more than herself. She came to know that you love the kids, but she can't give birth to a child. She doesn't want to snatch your happiness of having kids of your own, so she moved away from you."

Raj was shocked and said to himself, "Shit, what I did, why I told her about kids and how she thought that I loved kids more than her—she is my life, yaar."

Raj hugged Arjun and scolded him, "Why didn't you tell me anything? Why did you tell me so late? If you didn't come to London or the hospital, I wouldn't have come to know all these things, and I could have lost Nidhi for life. You know, I love her so much. why you didn't told me yar."

Arjun: "Sorry, she told me not to tell anything to you."

Raj hugged him happily and said, You made my life. I will go to her now only and will slap her and scold her.

Arjun: "Don't dare to slap her, ok."

Raj: "Arre yar, don't worry, I will hug her and scold her for wasting my whole 3 years of my life."

Both of them laughed and said, I will go now to bring her. Arjun, she won't agree so easily; we have to plan something else.

Arjun: "Raj, go and prepare your engagement ceremony."

Raj: "What?"

Arjun: "Just do what I say."

Both called everyone and said the good news. Everyone was very happy, and they shared their plan with each other. According to the plan, Raj called Nidhi and said, "My marriage got fixed, so please come to my engagement ceremony. I know you don't want to come, but as you told me, you don't love me, so as a good friend, come to the function. I will feel happy and will send the venue."

Nidhi: "Congratulations, I definitely come as your good friend."

As she cut the call, she started to cry. Rahim consoled her. They both went to Mumbai, as their function was arranged in their home only. So she went to his home, and the function is on the next day, but her parents told her to come to his home only, so she came there. All her friends were already standing there. She greeted everyone. Searching for a bride, she saw that girl touching Raj and correcting his dress. By seeing all this, she felt irritation, so she decided to move out. Her friends stopped her and said, "You only wanted him to move on, so finally he moved on, leaving you behind as his memory."

Everyone stayed there only as the function was on the next day; each of them stayed in Raj's place.

At night, as per their plan, Raj went to talk with Nidhi.

Raj: "I still love you, so I want to propose to you once again. Want to do a second try? Please come into my life."

Nidhi: "No, I don't love you."

Raj: "Then why do you get irritated when someone comes near to me or when they touch me? Why are you crying then? Why are you jealous? Why are you still single?"

Nidhi: "What you are talking about, I didn't get any jealous or didn't cry; why should I? You just misunderstood the things."

Raj called everyone there and said, "You all lied to me that she loves me, but she is not agreeing."

Nidhi was shocked to see them there and said, "No, I don't love you."

Everyone said, "Please agree that you love him; we know that."

Rahim: "Then why do you still keep his photo with you? Why did you cry when he called you? You remember, na, that you scolded me for talking wrong about him."

Everyone was forcing her to say it, yar.

Nidhi shouted at them, "Ha, I love him, still loving." Raj immediately hugged her and said, "I love you too." Nidhi pushed him and said, "I can't marry you."

Raj: "What? But why?"

Nidhi: "I don't deserve you. If you marry me, then you don't get anything."

Raj: "You are my life, yar. When you are with me, I feel like all happiness is with me."

Nidhi: "Why are you not understanding that I can't give you that happiness, which you dreamt of, for which you already planned many things? I can't give you a child, yar. Try to understand the fact that I can't marry you."

Raj: "I know it."

Nidhi was shocked and said, "What?"

Nidhi: "By knowing all these things, still you want to marry me?"

Raj: "It doesn't matter to me, yar, how you thought that I stopped loving you after knowing this thing; you matter to me more than any child; you are more important to me than the child, which is not even there in this world."

Raj: "Ha, I want children, but not with another woman. That time I told you indirectly that I want to make children with you, not like they are more important to me than anything else."

Raj: "If I really wanted kids, I could have married someone else without waiting for you. How could you think all these years, almost 3 years, that if you marry me, then you will snatch my happiness? You know by moving away from me you snatched my life, yar; my happiness lies with you."

Raj: "You didn't realize that how I led my life all these 3 years without you, I didn't attend any functions or any parties, didn't smile with anyone, didn't sing a song, or didn't dance until and unless I met you. When you sang a song, I sang; when you danced, I danced, seeing you do that too at Arjun's marriage. Now you decide what is important to me, you or a child who is not even on Earth. Why are you standing quietly? Answer me."

Nidhi just stood there in full shock by hearing his words. Again Raj said, "You know, Arjun told me to think about my parents. But your impact on them was so much that even though they didn't select any girl, instead they were comparing every girl with you and then rejected them.

Raj: "When I told them all these things, my mom started to cry for your condition, and Pappa got angry and wanted to come to you at that time and wanted to scold you, slap you, and bring you directly to Mumbai. In fact, they just need you in their life, not anything else. Why are you so stubborn, yar? Please come into my life again and make me live in that again, filling happiness in our life once again." He sat down on his knees.

Nidhi started to cry and saw everyone's face, and they were all telling her to say yes. Nidhi went to him and hugged him tightly. Everyone started to clap for them and was happy for both. Nidhi and Raj's parents hugged each other as they stayed outside the room.

Raj: "Guys, now I am going to propose to my would-be wife. Cheer me on, guys."

Everyone was shouting and supporting him and said, "Come on, Raj, don't leave her today."

He just sat on his knees and said, I proposed to you already. I want to propose to you once again, "Will you marry me? Will you be my better half?"

Everyone is waiting for Nidhi's answer, everyone including those shouting at her to say yes. Nidhi: "Ok, I will answer. Before that, I want to meet Uncle and Auntie."

She went to them and asked, "Please say it frankly that you both really want me as your daughter-in-law despite knowing all my things."

His mother said, "No, I don't accept you as my daughter-in-law, but as my daughter, don't have any second thoughts that we agreed because he loves you, but the truth is before him we already decided to make you my daughter-in-law; in fact, we both decided that if he didn't agree to that, we would slap him and make him marry you, but by God's grace he loves you."

His father said, "Don't have any second thoughts. Who told you that we can't be grandparents? We already became grandparents when Rahim called us his grandparents when we met him today, so don't worry about anything. One thing I learned when I met you is that sometimes the relationships that are from the heart are stronger than blood relationships. You only taught me this, so why are you behaving like this? Please come to our life; we are fed up with his boring life."

Nidhi just hugged them and started to cry. Arjun: "Nidhi, sometimes bad things happen for a good reason only. Maybe God wants you to share your love with the world; it should not be limited to your child, so only he planned like this; otherwise, we should have shared your love with your kid. Many fights may happen, so to be on the safer side, it is good only."

Rahim: I used to call you Ridhima, but today, from this minute, I will call you "maa."

Adopted Granny and his wife came and said, "You have a mother's heart, so only you took care of me as a mother. Who says you don't have kids? We are here, na."

Ajay: "You treated every one of us like your brother and sister; this means you are not less than Mom, na."

Everyone said, "You are the bright star of our life. Whenever we have problems, we call you so that you will help us in any manner. We trust you as we trust our moms blindly. Everyone convinced her that she didn't lose anything; she is more special to them.

Nidhi looked at everyone and said, "Why should I cry? She has such beautiful relationships in her life; each one of them loves her so much that she doesn't get time to think of any child in her life. She has to handle many relationships in her life; she loves to handle it." Everyone was smiling at her.

But Raj is still waiting for her answer: "Arre yar, stop it yar. I am waiting for her answer now; don't make her emotional now."

Nidhi laughed at him and said, "Ha, yes, for your every proposal."

Everyone got happy and hugged each other and started to distribute the sweets. Nidhi's father came to her and said, "Now I've got to know what you have earned in your life. I'm a really proud father."

Nidhi "Pappa, all these because of your upbringing and the trust you have in me, you trusted me and gave me independence to do what I wanted to, allowed me to roam with friends, allowed me to go out at night, gave me money, and told me how to use it wisely. Everything you taught me is the foundation of this beautiful life. If every father understands their daughter, then she will be the strongest one, Pappa. Love you. In fact, I got god-gifted friends who didn't misuse me."

Suddenly she realized something and asked everyone, "What about the engagement party, and what about that girl?"

Everyone laughed at her and said, "That girl is our employee, and this function is for Raj's and your engagement party, and it's a fully planned one."

Nidhi suddenly called Raj at the corner and asked, "How could you allow her to touch you? How dare you do that? How many girls did you like this"?

Raj: "My Nidhi is back." Hugged her tightly and said, "She is my cousin sister working in my company; it's just drama. No one has the guts to touch Nidhi's boyfriend."

Nidhi smiled and felt shy. She started to move, but he held her and said, "You didn't say those beautiful and magical three words."

Nidhi: "You have. To wait for that" and went off.

At night at the dining table, Nidhi said, "Love you guys. From now on, I don't cry about what I don't have because I have many relationships to handle. Love you all for this big support."

Abhi: "Meri positive wali Radha is back."

At the engagement party, they both exchanged their rings. Abhi said, "Radha ko Krishna mil gaya."

Abhi and Anusha were doing some research on Nidhi's condition. Without others knowledge. At the party, their parents told them about their planning and what they made before their London plan, and everyone was shocked and all were happy for that.

The next day, Nidhi asked Raj to come with her to Delhi. They went there and met ashram people. She introduced Raj to everyone, and everyone asked her whether he is the person whom she loves.

Raj: "Whether they know everything."

Nidhi: "My life is like an open book; they know everything of my life."

Raj: "So except for me, everyone in this world knows that you love me."

Nidhi smiled at him and hugged him. Everyone treated him so well that he is like their son-in-law and told him to take care of Nidhi.

Raj: "I will promise that I don't give any chance to point me."

They left from there. And he asked her that they have to change the records of Rahim. Nidhi, we should do it after marriage, when you become my husband.

Nidhi: "You are everything to me."

After that, they went to the adoptive parents as they entered there; even they were treated in the same manner and asked about the marriage date. Nidhi said it's next month. Baba said, "Ok, then select your designs now so that I can make them before your marriage."

Nidhi: "But one condition: you have to take money, except for jumkis."

Baba: "How is it possible?"

Nidhi: "Ok, then we are leaving."

Baba: "Ok, I will, but you have to take my gift, whatever I give you."

Nidhi "Only your love and blessings are enough; only those jhumkas I will take."

Baba: "Ok."

Nidhi: "For selecting designs, I will come with my gang."

After that, they went to Mumbai. After reaching there, Nidhi went to Bangalore. Their marriage will be next month itself, and it's arranged in Bangalore only, so. In Bangalore, while her whole gang is busy scheduling the functions and required arrangements, Nidhi is busy inviting each and every friend of hers, as there is only one month remaining. Some are busy in their work, but some are in Bangalore only for Nidhi's help. Arjun, Ajay, Arpita, and her Salman bhai stay with Nidhi. Ankit and Anjali, who are busy with their work, will join them very soon. Abhi and Nidhi went to meet all their bands, who all worked with them in Delhi, and invited them to their marriage. Nidhi told them that" You all are invited as my special friends, not as a band to perform."

They said, "This makes you special and different from others, as everyone invited us but told us to perform. In fact, our families did the same. Love you, Nidhi, and we will come."

Personally, she went everywhere to invite everyone in Delhi. They went to the ashram and invited everyone and said, "I booked a train. Whoever can travel can come. If anyone has a problem coming, then please don't take a risk. I will come here after my marriage to take blessings from you." Everyone felt happy that she was inviting us as her family members; they said they will come. Daily Raj used to call her, and every time she was busy with her work.

In Bangalore, Arjun, his wife, Ajay, and Arpita decided to do shopping for Nidhi, as she said to them that each and every costume should be chosen by them, and in fact, jewellery also, as she selected jewellery for them, so now it's their turn. Everyone is so busy that they handle everything themselves without any selfishness. This is what Nidhi means to them. But our Raja is getting so much irritation that he can't be able to talk with her.

Raj thought to call her at midnight. He called, but she was already sleeping. Many times he called, and finally Nidhi woke up and received the call. "Sorry, I was busy with some work."

Raj: "Tomorrow we are going to London to invite everyone there. I already booked your tickets to Mumbai and from here to London."

Nidhi: "How is it possible for me? Please, you only invite them on my behalf."

Raj: "No, you have to come with me. I already spoke with Uncle and took permission from them; you're just coming". and cut the call.

Nidhi got to know that he was angry, went to her parents in the morning, and said that Raj's plan, as they already knew about it, was just yes, and said, "Enjoy your day." Nidhi went to Mumbai. As she reached him, she hugged him and said, Sorry.

Raj: "Okay, come on, it's getting late."

They went to London. He was in an angry mood only. As they entered their home, she was invited by his workers. " They said, "Welcome to our future owner."

Nidhi smiled at them, as they had a lot of work, and their returning flight was at midnight only, so they rushed out to invite everyone, first the office, then the college and hostel, and next the police, who helped her once. Later, they came home. After dinner, he took her to that room and showed her. She was surprised to see that the full room was filled with her pics only. She got to know how much he missed her in the past 3 years. She got down on her knees and asked, "Will you give me another chance to enter your life? Will you give permission to add some other photos in this room, in fact, our marriage photos? She started to say all silly things."

Raj smiled at her and said, "Yes."

Nidhi: "I love you, Raj."

Raj happily hugged her and said, "For this to happen, he took her here. After this they went back to India. From the airport, she decided to go to Bangalore directly and promised Raj that she would call him once a day despite her busy schedule.

As the marriage date is near, everyone came there, and all are busy with the work of the marriage.

{Now a beautiful marriage started finally… This marriage is very special because here, they are not blood relatives; most of them are related to Nidhi, whom she loves from the heart. Heart relationships are stronger than blood relations. Here, as a writer, I am not saying this is good and that is bad; I am just saying sometimes other relations become stronger than blood relations. If we see Nidhi's life, it looks true, because in these functions, most of them are related to Nidhi and her personality; they handle all rituals from their heart, some working as a brother, some as her grannies, and some as her best friend. In that all are not Hindu but are handling all rituals like it's their religion and are taking part in Hindu rituals as their own, no caste discrimination—awesome. Now, this is what I want to tell through my story.

Finally her marriage started, something the same as a fair. Each and every person came there just to bless her. From outside, if we see that function, it looks like some fair is going on; so many people are present. By seeing all this, Raj smiled and said that he is marrying a girl who is a sister to many, a daughter to many, a granddaughter to many, and a guiding instructor for many people. For some, she is everything to their life, like Arjun; he just watches everyone and feels proud of her.

After Pooja, there is one ritual to tie the knot for couples. Swami called any family member to come forward and do that ritual. He was shocked to see that a total of 10 people came over there, like Ankit and

Anjali, Abhi and Anusha, Arjun and his wife, Geet, Ajay and Arpita, and Rahim, who holds a special place in her life. Raj was surprised and looked at Nidhi.

Nidhi: "I told everyone who and which ritual they should do."

While Kanyadhana totals 6 people, it, like Nidhi's parents, adopted Baa and his wife and Ajay's parents. Even she called Arjun's father, but he refused it as it's couples work, so later he came there and blessed her.

Ajay, Salman, Ankit, and Arpita's brother did every ritual that should be done by brothers.

After tying the mangalsutra, Raj smiled at her and said, "You're mine now, only mine."

Nidhi: "You too. We both together will make this life more beautiful."

After this, there is another ritual where Nidhi's father has to wash the groom's feet. Arjun's father came to the front as she told him to do that ritual. Raj refused to do that; everyone told him it's just a ritual—he had to do that. As it finished, he touched his uncle's feet and took blessings. After this, they took blessings from each and every elder there.

After that, they got ready and went to the stage. Everyone came there and gave their blessing to the couple. Both of them, without any tiredness, took photos with each and every person. All from the ashram and school were present there. By seeing all of them, Nidhi felt very happy.

At the same time, all her friends and all the bands decided to give her a surprise; they started to sing a song that was made by her as their theme song.

{One different thing is every band competes with each other as rivals outside the function hall, but they all sing together, singing for her as a single group; that is Nidhi's marriage specialty.}

They all came to Nidhi gave the mic to her to sing; she joined, and even Raj started to join, so he played guitar.

Every guest was impressed by this scene after the song's completion, as they all came to the stage to take a photo. Nidhi scolded them for singing, as she wanted them to enjoy the function; she didn't want them to perform or showcase their talent for free. They said, "We didn't perform; we gifted you in this mode. That's it." She smiled by hearing that and said, "Thank you for your wonderful gift."

Now it's time for her gang to enter the stage, as she told them before that she doesn't need any gifts; in fact, she ordered them. So they made a short film and gave it to her, which included her life story, from her birth to marriage with Raj, her friends, how it started, how it became stronger, how she met Raj, some good moments, some bad, and told her to watch it later.

Finally all the functions were over, and all of them sat in the big hall to get a group photo. After that, they watched that video, and she got emotional after watching that. She hugged them for this beautiful, valuable, and unmatched gift and said, "You all are my best buddies." The photographer captured that moment. In fact, Nidhi kept the photographer and video guy in her home only the past 15 days so that they wouldn't miss any moment of her marriage. Guess how many albums there will be for only one marriage. That is Nidhi, who sees life from a different angle.

She saw everyone from the stairs and thought about their journey from birth to date, how many bad and good moments, and how all relations joined in her journey. Finally, all went to their cities for their work; they all got busy in their day-to-day lives. But all are in touch with each other through Nidhi's habit of calling daily at night.

After some days, Abhi got a medal for his research in the medical field, Arjun is happily living with his wife, Ajay and Arpita are busy with their family planning, Ankit and Anjali got married, Geet is busy in her own life, Rahim continued his studies, and Anusha is busy with her doctoring.

After two years, Nidhi is sitting with her marriage album, seeing how Arjun is pulling his wife's pallu, Abhi flirting with her, how her parents are watching her with tears, how grannies are taking care of her and pulling her leg, Ankit and Anjali romancing, Anusha taking care of everyone, and how Salman Bhai's mom is feeding her favourite sweet to her. She is just recalling everything and smiling to herself.

Suddenly Raj called, "Come to Avni and Arnav's school, as a parents' meeting is there."

{All are shocked, na. Who are Avni and Arnav? They are twins adopted by Raj and Nidhi; they have three children.}

Many things changed in these two years. Rahim joined his own company as an employee, as his mother, Nidhi, is the number one fashion designer now; Raj, doing his best in his life, became the topmost businessman in the world; Arjun and his wife handling their business, Nishi opened many orphanages; Abhi and Anusha now have a cute baby girl and have their own hospital; Ajay and Arpita are handling the Bangalore office as they were named as its CEO; Ankit joined IIM as a lecturer, and Anjali joined some company. All their parents decide to stay in Bangalore in the same home, enjoying their life with bindass. Salman bhai is the owner of many taxis.

Everyone settled in their life; only one thing didn't change: that is the love between them.

Nidhi didn't stop her work towards the society; she handled everything. Everything can change; only one girl doesn't change, and that is Nidhi.

Abhi's research helped Nidhi to get a child of her own. As I told you, he is busy with some research; he even got a medal for that, so he proved it experimentally and made Nidhi's life full of happiness. He translated uterus of someone to Nidhi.

{ God just tests us, but finally he will give us what is better for us. He can't be so cruel to Nidhi, who led her whole life without selfishness, without hurting anyone. He just wants to give everything good at the right time, so sometimes God will make delays for some things for giving good things}.

The end

This might be the end of my story, but not for their life....

"Agar Nidhi ke jaisa zindagi jeena hai toh

zindagi ko kul ke jio yar, kya pata kal ho na ho."

Just keep smiling.

"At last, one thing: If we respect a girl/woman, she will give everything, every type of happiness, for us for that little respect. So please respect a woman who gave birth to you and one who filled your life with happiness as a sister, mother, daughter, wife, friend, and everything. Respect her, love her, and then definitely you will get another Nidhi in your life ..."

Shraxmi

www.ingramcontent.com/pod-product-compliance
Lightning Source LLC
Chambersburg PA
CBHW031332130726
47988CB00007B/3095